ETERNALLY BELOVED:

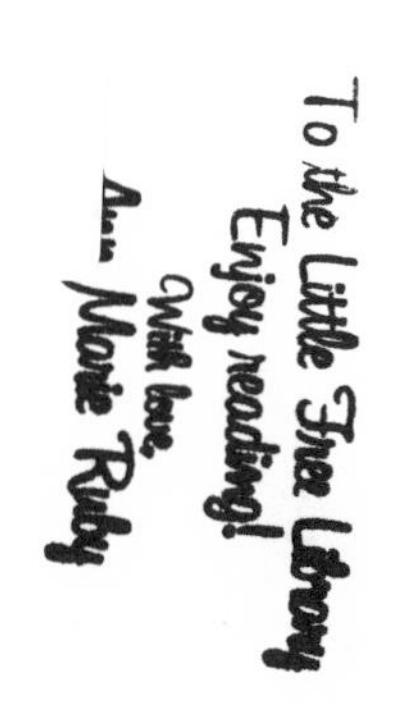

I SHALL NEVER LET YOU GO

BOOK ONE OF THE *KASTEEL VREDERIC* SERIES

"Love lives on forever even though life ends at death. Yet love with her wagon of immortality makes true lovers immortal."

Ann Marie Ruby

Copyright © 2021 Ann Marie Ruby

All rights reserved. No part of this book may be reproduced in any form or stored in any retrieval system without prior written permission from the publisher. Book cover images are composed of stock photos from istockphoto.com and/or specifically illustrated for this book. Interior images are composed of stock photos from istockphoto.com, stock photos released under CC0 from Pixabay.com, and/or specifically illustrated for this book.

Disclaimer:

This book ("***Eternally Beloved: I Shall Never Let You Go***") in no way represents or endorses any religious, philosophical, political, or scientific view. It has been written in good faith for people of all cultures and beliefs. This book has been written in American English. There may be minor variations in the spelling of names and dates due to translations from Dutch, provincial languages, and regional dialects, or minor discrepancies in historical records.

This is a work of historical romance fiction framed within the true Eighty Years' War which took place in the Netherlands. Any resemblance to actual persons, living or dead, is purely coincidental. While the Netherlands, her cities, towns, and villages are real, references to historical events, real people, or real locations are used fictitiously.

Published in the United States of America, 2021.

ISBN-10: 0-578-84914-3

ISBN-13: 978-0-578-84914-0

DEDICATION

"In life or in death, twin flames are eternally one throughout time."

Love is a magical spell that showers the physical and spiritual soul. Bathed in the magical rain showers of a love spell, two minds, bodies, and souls become one. Born as an individual yet incomplete without the beloved for true lovers are only complete when united within one another.

The heart beats until the body is no more, yet what happens when your twin flame's heartbeat stops? Does your heartbeat stop too? How can you the individual go on when your other half is no more?

Love is eternal. Love lives on even after the last breath. Love proves two minds, bodies, and souls become one within the eternal love stories. Love never dies as long as the lovers keep the sacred love stories buried within their inner souls.

This book was framed within the historic Eighty Years' War. During this period, a lot of soldiers and civilians had lost their lives. They lost their lives to bring peace, love, and joy back to the lives and land they loved. Lives and livelihoods of soldiers and innocent civilians were sacrificed during the Eighty Years' War. Such is the result of all wars.

I dedicate this eternal love story to all the war victims of the Eighty Years' War of the Netherlands. I know the victims of this war will be remembered throughout time. Yet

I wonder how many victims were separated from their beloved family members because of the war.

My fictional characters represent soldiers, fathers, mothers, grandparents, beloved lovers, and children who were affected by the Eighty Years' War. So, I would like to remember all the civilians, soldiers, and those of you who have found a place in the books of history. Never shall I forget those of you who were lost within the pages of memory lane due to no recorded diaries found. Your stories are recorded through the memories of the mouth-to-mouth storytellers.

Today through my pen and paper, I have written one such fictional story that has no record of ever being in existence. All of you who had existed yet were not recorded shall be remembered, just like all of you who were recorded shall also exist within my inner soul. Through my love, I have found a place for all of you not in the pages of history but within my inner love.

With all my love, I dedicate this book and the following poem to all victims of the Eighty Years' War. I believe even when all is lost, love lives on between two lovers, between a land and her citizens, and between you the victims of a war and I the one who honors you. The poem, from my book *Love Letters: The Timeless Treasure*, is as follows,

NEVER LET YOU GO

Forever love survives on.

Forever love is youthful.

You and I grow old,

Yet our love only grows in depth,

And remains young throughout time.

Eras shall pass,

And time shall bid her farewell.

Remember my love,

Even when you are old,

And I am frail,

Hold on to me for support.

For even then, I shall

Hold on to you for support.

For even then,

Keep me within your inner soul,

As I shall forever keep you in my soul.

For if ever,

My mind and body fail,

Even then forever,

I shall grasp on to our love and you,

For a promise made to you my love is,

I shall

***NEVER LET YOU GO*.**

MESSAGE FROM THE AUTHOR

"Even when nothing is left, may my love for you and your love for me tie us in union eternally."

Four centuries and fifty-three years ago, from 1568 to 1648, the Netherlands had fought the Eighty Years' War for independence. They sought independence from Spanish rulers and freedom from religious persecution. During this period, the Netherlands was known as the Spanish Netherlands, and some parts were known as the Dutch Republic.

After a long and hard-fought battle against Spain, the Netherlands found her sovereignty. The Netherlands became independent in 1648. I will throughout this book refer to this land as the Netherlands, out of respect for a country which had fought a hard and bloody war for her independence.

Yet how many stories do we know from that time period? What about the human nightingales who had called on one another, throughout the dark and war-filled nights? What if a pair of human lovebirds were calling for one another from beyond the enemy line?

Come travel time with me and from beyond the clouds, watch a couple unite even beyond time and tide. Within the pages of this book, I have united true love not fearing even death. Who says death separates, for I say nothing can separate true love as long as you believe.

Believe in true love and the first and last vows of twin flames. To bring back belief and faith in the power of twin flames, again I have taken my pen to paper. Through the pages of this book, I will bring back upon this Earth true twin flames and the vows of eternal love.

Fall in love again with your twin flame as you walk through the lives of eternal twin flames. Nothing prevented them from falling in love, not even the worst enemy of all humans known as time. This book is a timeless love story which shall flow from shore to shore as eternally yours.

Come travel time with me as I introduce you to a war-ravaged era, where even the fear of persecution did not prevent love traveling from heart to heart. Maybe as you get acquainted with these legendary figures and listen to their stories, you will see how they will inspire you to believe in true love, and that love does live on even beyond time.

TABLE OF CONTENTS

PROLOGUE

"Let the clouds upon the skies open the curtains for you. It is then you shall get a glimpse of a story that had begun and ended, before it even had a chance."

Jacobus van Vrederic, in his private study.

Thunderclouds have brought rain, lightning, and thunder over the huge castle in Naarden, the Netherlands. The locals know this castle as Kasteel Vrederic, named after my forefathers. I ask myself why Mother Nature would show her temper and anger with such loud noises. In love and war, a person should never show his or her temper for then, you give out your identity to your enemies.

I didn't have any practical experiences as I had chosen to hide from the realities of life. Avoiding rumors, neglecting all others, and always putting myself first had made a lonely old man out of me. Rejecting my only love, rejecting my only child, and rejecting a life outside of this stone fortress had gifted me with a lifelong prison sentence within the walls of a dark castle. Rejected not from my mind, body, or soul, but I was forced to by fear for my beloved's life.

This dark home has vines growing all over and a very well-kept garden with well-kept boxwoods creating the borders for various exotic flowering beds. The only thing this fortress could not grow or plant was love, or allow to be loved. This is an acquired characteristic I spent my entire life to change.

All the heavenly flowers covering this home still make it look like a forbidden fortress. I am the selfish, very well-disciplined, hardworking, and cold narrator of my diary. For all of you who will visit the pages of my diary, do try to forgive me if you can only find some forgiveness within your inner soul.

The story I shall retell to all of you started off with my life and affected my only child, whom I never met in this life. At least, not until we were separated by a breath. A father's only child, the musical blessing for a musician, and the love of his beloved, all came to an end like the sunset marking the end of a day.

Walk with me to a fairytale garden not far from this cold fortress. In this magical garden, within their final resting place, sleep two young lovebirds. For them, I have gifted all the flowers a human could dream of. The flowers are very well pruned. They are always awake, even though the people they guard are asleep.

These lovebirds are covered from the cold chilling rain and the scorching heated sun as I have kept them protected under the huge birch trees. I could not protect them while they were awake. So, I tried to do my best as they forever peacefully lay asleep. The musical birds come and visit them as I have invited all musical birds to sing to them, quietly throughout the days and throughout the nights.

The nightfall streams light from the glorious moon as she sends the reflections onto the reflecting river waters, flowing throughout time. The magical portrait of true love is found here, except the forever lovers don't talk or wake up. I have requested the clouds to cover them and give them some privacy. These lovebirds don't talk with me, yet I talk to them.

Let me read to you their everlasting love story from my diary. For then you too will get to know them and can retell their love story to all across this globe throughout time. You must travel time and travel to a country which had fought years for her independence.

Willem van Oranje had declared war to get freedom and independence of the Netherlands from Spain. We, the Dutch people, speak Dutch and have similar ancestry as we are of the West Germanic ethnicity. During this war, so many stories have been written. Yet this love story got lost as this is hidden within my personal diary.

Today though, I have opened the pages of my diary to read for you an eternal love story. Come with me and travel through the pages of my diary as I take you through the wagon of time and land in 1572. I will take you to a time when simple social differences between a woman and a man prevented true twin flames who were made for one another from uniting, not by themselves but by societal grouches. Against them was also the biggest enemy known to all humans which is and shall always be time.

Even when all things are working in your favor, you still have to hope time does not become your enemy. All things in life must be accomplished within one's heartbeat, so they are not separated by a breath. The harsh reality is time is not merciful to even twin flames. The tear fall creates an ocean and a waterfall yet still cannot freeze time. Only memories freeze within the memory beholder's inner diary.

I will tell you of a story how a father had said his final farewell to his beloved daughter. I am Jacobus van Vrederic, father of the bride who became a bride, however, I never had the fortune to give her away as a bride. Never did I get to see her during her stay on Earth, as we were separated by a breath.

Today, however, I had bid my farewell to her and her eternal twin flame. As you get introduced to these magical lovebirds of an enchanted garden, I will also share my personal love story where my eternally beloved never found a grave but a memorial garden for our daughter and her twin flame.

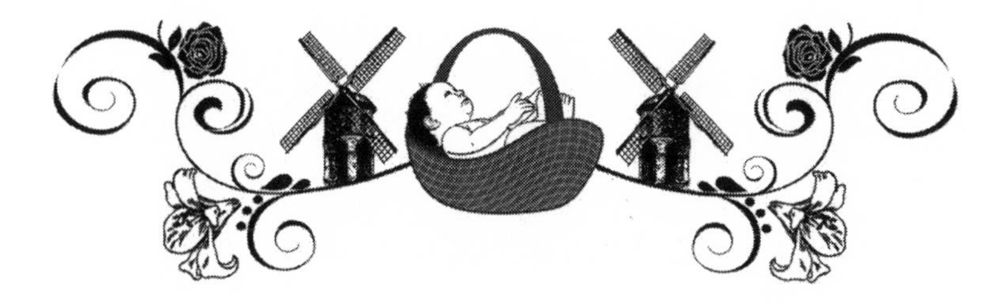

CHAPTER ONE:

A FATHER'S CONSTRAINT

"The ability to begin and end a story does not justify the action and the ultimate reaction."

Fisherman Altfrit van Visser, entering Kasteel Vrederic with baby Griet.

Unrest and war had begun in the sixteenth century, in the Netherlands. The Dutch nobleman, Willem van Oranje, had asked the Spanish local authorities to stop the persecution of the Protestants. Yet the war continued. Lands were won and then land after land was lost as were lives. There was fire burning everywhere, where the Protestants and the Catholics fought one another.

This night was not different for there were sounds of war going on as Mother Nature too was fierce outside. She displayed forever her power was so much more superior than any war. At times, however, she displayed her motherly side too.

She filled the air with thunder, lightning, and heavy rain. The fearful storm was not favored by some people I had loved with all my heart. Others like myself, however, enjoyed the unrest outside as it comforted the unrest and storm brewing within me.

The son of a landowner I am, who acquired a castle, name, fame, and power. Not preferential by others though I did have a temper like the ravaging storm outside. I never showed my temper as I kept all of it buried within my soul.

A knock on my heavy wooden doors jerked me back to reality. The castle guard had approached me as he had a stranger with him. The stranger waiting at the door was scared of voicing his words. I wanted to comfort him and let him know I am not a scary person. Say whatever you need to say. Yet I said nothing and his fear of me never eased.

In between us was just an uncomfortable silence as time stood still. The stranger had within his hands a weathered fisherman's basket. I could smell fish in the air. As I monitored the man's hands, I knew he was a fisherman by trade. No one spoke as they all wanted my permission to speak.

So, I asked, "Who are you and what do you want at this late hour of the night? No one knocks or has the audacity to come to my home this late in the night."

I should have been softer and asked if he wanted someone to talk to, for I sure could have someone to talk to. But my attitude of not saying anything so I can hide my emotions, came into place. I saw in the mirror looking back at myself was my mirror image, a very arrogant man, six feet tall.

I always wore dark clothing. I guess it matched my emotionless self-centered personality. Or I tried to cover up my emotions as I always wore a cloak on top of my attire. I never shaved off my French beard as my Margriete loved my beard and always asked me to stay clean and tidy up. For my love, I would keep up my beard, bathe, clean, and tidy up the outer me. Yet how would I settle the inner self?

My unwanted guest replied, “Sir, I have no want or need to disturb you, but I have a basket left by a woman with a note for you. I am a fisherman and a Protestant. I come in peace. My name is Altfrit van Visser. My wife lives near you in Naarden. She was a good friend of the Catholic nun Agatha who had been your childhood educator and help until her death.”

I imagined what could be in the basket, maybe fresh baked bread or fish. He continued, “I have brought you something that was left at my cottage by the lake, by a Catholic nun. She told me to bring it quietly and to make sure no one sees this. I would have preferred to wait till dawn but then I would bring rumors and unwanted conversations to town.”

Then, suddenly like the relentless storm outside, the quiet and peaceful air inside tore through the cries of a baby. I lost my temper. Like a furious and angry man, I shouted back at the innocent fisherman. I knew no one would come and visit my family home unless it was urgent.

Never giving priority to the other person's feelings, or even being sympathetic, I shouted at him, "How dare you bring a young child to my home in the middle of the night! I have a very temperamental elderly father who would be disturbed by your game. This would not be good for you."

The open windows started to bring in rough, forceful winds trying to warn me of a future I might regret. A lonely future, where this sweet cry would have been music to my ears. My temper got the better of me until I saw a note that was left with the basket.

All my inner fear disappeared as I could almost hear a certain voice. I felt a certain feeling of unconditional love. A small woman's unconditional giving flooded back waking a certain part of my inner soul I had tried so hard to close off.

I knew the untidy handwriting so well. A very petite woman, five feet, four inches in height, with brown hair and fair skin was smiling back at me. A very poor yet beautiful housemaid whom I loved like a madman, watched me from the windows of my memories.

I could hear her laughter. I could feel her soft skin. I could touch her soft silky hair. I wanted to hold on to her and forget the harsh reality of her not being here.

My thoughts were silenced off by the fisherman's voice, "This was left for you, sir. Maybe this will give you some clues as to the mystery behind this child. She was left here in good condition. The nuns from the church told me she came with a letter addressed to you. It said private, so I left it unopened."

I looked at the letter and wanted to smell the paper. I wanted to place the paper in my heart where no one would see it but only my eyes. I knew who the author of the letter was. I felt the Earth around me shake and we were left amongst an earthquake.

That's when my father, Johannes van Vrederic, walked in with his cigar. He was always outfitted in a very rich-looking, clean, and majestical doublet that talked about his fortune and status. He always smelled like expensive cigars and he never allowed anyone near his inner self.

My father was six feet, five inches tall. He was a very slim and fit man. His hair was short and dark brown. My father had a clean French beard. His skin color was paler, as a direct effect of his travels.

I realized he had aged rather faster in the last few years. My father never spoke of his past, yet everyone knew something happened when he had traveled with the Portuguese merchants to India. I was brought home as a small child who never knew his Indian mother.

Maybe that's why I became such an introvert. Or maybe because I never had a father place a kiss on my cheek as I went to bed alone. Or I never had a father sit and dine with me, as I had dined alone with my nannies.

My father spoke authoritatively with his deep and fearful voice, "Jacobus, this basket is a mistake and must leave the castle before it makes any noise. I will handle this situation. You should only worry about keeping the family honor. Like I said to you earlier, this is a family dishonor which I will not allow in the house. Whatever is in the basket will never enter this home alive!"

I dreaded the cigar my father always had. It had created an enmity with my inner being. I had dreaded the smell of cigars ever since the day I found out how ruthless of a person my father was. I linked him to cigars always.

I was silent and walked out without a word. The inside of my entire being froze. I prayed to my Lord for help. I thought if the thing in the basket can never enter the home alive, then may it never enter the home. I knew the thing he so calls it by was the symbol of my lost love. I wanted the thing to live at any cost, even if it meant it must be kept far away from me.

I followed and spoke with the fisherman as he was about to leave. I asked the fisherman, "How much would you charge to not kill the child and give it to the nuns to raise? I will keep paying you and the nuns for it, as long as you let it live. I don't want it to come close to this home or anyone in this home."

The fisherman smiled at me and said, "I will not charge you anything as this is not an 'it' but she, and she is a child of God. I hope the nuns can take care of her, but the church has been burned down."

He paused and continued, "All the people inside of the church have either died or left. The war is merciless and is taking all on its way."

I felt like I just died inside. I prayed for a very petite woman who I wanted to stay as far away from me as she could. Not for myself but so she lives and finds love eternally. I would sacrifice anything in this world to only know she was well and safe. I kept on praying, may you be safe and be mine even far away from me. I could still hear the wishes of a very petite young woman saying, "Promise you will never let me go." I wanted the fisherman to say the mother of the baby fled far away from the war and was safe.

My thoughts suddenly broke as the fisherman said, "I will take care of her. Don't worry about her. I just wanted you to know, her mother was burned to death during the fire that burned down the church. No bodies were found, however, it was assumed all must have died. The nuns were able to save the child but not the mother. I will take her away from here and I give you my oath, she will never enter this home. Please keep the letter, as this was the last gift left for you by her mother."

The fisherman had left. Yet I felt he wanted to say something but did not. After a while, he second guessed and turned around.

He came back and asked, "Are you sure you don't even want to see her once? Maybe give her your blessing to have a nice life. It will be a hard life as even my wife who wants to raise her does not want to touch her as everyone says she is untouchable. She looks like a mystical princess. I will try to give her a good life."

I told him, “No, it’s better I don’t see her. Maybe one day if time allows us to meet, I will see her. I want my child to live and not be buried in childhood by unjust humans.”

I kept hearing her mother’s voice pleading me to never let her go. I feared not anything but for the life of my child. I knew within the walls of this cold fortress was an old man who would not hesitate to take the life of my young daughter to save his own honor in the eyes of his so-called society.

I never got to see the child whom I had sired with the love of my life. I could not even honor my love as she was a poor village girl with whom I had made love. I felt like I rejected her when she needed me the most. I distanced her from myself, only to protect her from my vile father and his threats of harming her.

I did not fear for myself but if my love for a woman would have caused the life of that certain woman, in the hands of an evil societal wrongdoer. I kept her away from myself not because I did not love her, but because I loved her more than life in itself. Yet it seemed like my fears had come true as life in itself could not give us another chance as time was against us.

I let go of my love not to be away from her but to save her. I wanted to give her a chance to live. She was a maid in my father's home I fell head over heels for. She was my wedded wife as recorded within the eyes of the Creator, even if not in the eyes of society.

My love's only wish was to be with me even at her last breath. Her life was taken away by the status and the differences of a punishing society. I watched the fisherman take upon his shoulders a responsibility he did not start or was a part of.

Everything inside me was being torn into pieces, yet nothing came to my mouth. This was my journey and my actions. This was a father's constraint.

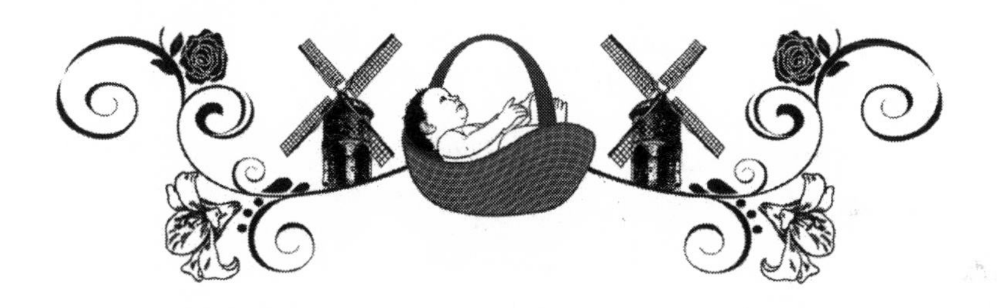

CHAPTER TWO:

LETTER FROM AN UNWED MOTHER

"Vow of an unwed made from the soul is not kept within the paper records on Earth, yet is it not honored and kept in the heart of the eternally beloved?"

Margriete van Wijck, preparing for her letter and baby to be delivered to Jacobus van Vrederic in the event something happens to her.

In 1572, Naarden was conquered by the Spanish troops. The dwellers of this city were shot in groups. I had survived as my family was able to escape this massacre. The church I refused to visit was burned down without mercy.

How did I not know the love of my life was hiding in the same church? The Catholic Church my family fought against, actually had helped my child see the first dawn on Earth. My child had opened her eyes to see dawn, yet this father's eyes never had the fate to see her eyes. Where was my child, the child I had refused to even take a glimpse at? I kept on hearing the small helpless cries of my child within my head.

Neither could I stop the sound, nor did I want to stop it, for it was the last gift of an unregistered father, a father she will never know or a child he will never hold. My hands wanted to touch my baby girl's warm cozy cheeks. Fear ripped through my inner core as I heard my father's ruthless curse.

I opened the last thread of linkage I had to my love. The lantern was lit as the fire waved and danced with the open window breeze. In the warmth and safety of this cold castle I lived, when I had no clue where my newborn child was.

I could feel the pain and hurt cut my inner core open. Yet like a coward, I froze again and refused to acknowledge my own feelings. The opinionated family honor had chained my feet and stopped my movements.

A very jealous and sacred lover, I wanted to keep my beloved's love letter hidden within my chest. Yet I will allow all to read it as love never dies but only grows as you retell the story. This world must read this love letter to grow within love. My beloved lives forever through her words, for my love survives even though I am like a living dead. Her letter read,

20th of November 1572

My Dear Eternally Beloved,

If this letter ever reaches you, then you must know I have gone to a place beyond time. Life without you was hard, but I am blessed to have had a life with you. The few days we had together became a lifetime as

time never ends where love survives. I have kept our united time forever blooming within my soul.

The wind blowing your brown hair is my prayer for you to always be happy. The sun glowing upon you is my smile blessing you from far away.

Forever, you shall find me when you need me through the miracle door of love. Today, I have left you with the proof of our union. She was born today, the 20th of November 1572, in this warzone.

I tried to hide with the nuns. They were ever so kind to allow a Protestant unwed mother to be with them.

Although things have become really dangerous for a single woman with a child, I will try to love our child and give her a good life as long as life allows.

The sisters at the church are really worried and have arranged a fisherman in Naarden to take our child to you in the case of my departure from this world. Your father had threatened all the nuns and the fishermen of this village to not take me or our child.

The fisherman who has agreed against your father's threats is a kind soul. He is a regular guest here and brings bread and fish for the church.

He and his wife have promised to take care of our daughter if and when needed.

My worry is even though we have wed in secrecy, our marriage is not acknowledged by society, as I have no paper proof. Proof of promissory vows and hidden oath in a church give no legitimacy to our legitimate child. She bears the shame of being illegitimate and unwanted.

I hope this world gives her a chance in life and love. May she find her love of life, like I had found you. As you are reading this letter, I hope you have found our love within your hands. Please keep her safe and know with her birth, our love has found its course.

I pray your father could agree and maybe raise her as a handmaiden in your household. Please ask him for his blessings and show him proof of our vows.

Forever I am yours. I know your father had told you I had passed away. Yet today when you do read this letter, it is now I have left this world. I pray if not in this life, then in the afterlife, I shall be yours again and forever.

Your Eternally Beloved,

Wedded Yet Unwed Wife,

Margriete van Wijck

I read and reread her scribbled handwriting. I could hear her sweet, soft voice talking to me. I wished I had the courage to walk out on my father and had held on to the love of my life. I told my father I would not accept his argument and wanted my daughter to be in the same home as her father.

I ran around the city looking for the sign of my lost love. I crossed rivers and cities on feet and on horse until I exhausted all my searches. I asked everyone about the child who survived the church fire. Days passed by and nights stormed by, yet again and again, I was told no one survived the church fire, not even a child.

My father passed away days after my child's departure. We never spoke as he was a very lonely man who never forgave himself for leaving my mother back in India. He had fallen in love with an Indian woman but could not let the world know he had married an Indian. His arrogance, or his unacceptance of another culture left him lonely for the rest of his life. I guess I was here in his household as I am a very European looking guy.

Never will I forgive my father for all the wrong he had done to a very innocent, soft-hearted soul. He had taken all of his cold-hearted social status revenge on an innocent woman. The wrong that was done unto him by his father for marrying a woman from a different culture, he had not forgotten or forgiven.

Instead of learning from his pain, he did the same thing his father had done unto him. He hunted down my Margriete and lied to all to keep his social status intact. What about two lives that were tied to one another and never had a chance to unite?

Like a stone, I froze and again fell prey to the harsh ways of social pressure. Never will I forget the love of my life. We were separated by the world yet forever I shall be yours in this world and beyond.

What is time to true lovers? I will wait out my time on Earth and unite with you within the ever after. Never did I wed again, because how could I wed another woman when I was forever wed to an unwed mother?

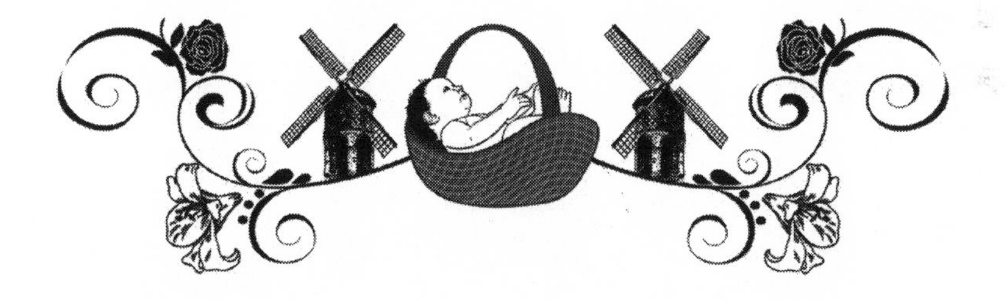

CHAPTER THREE:

THE MAID AND THE MASTER

"Falling in love with the other half you know completes you. Hitherto the social status of the unfair society separates you into half again."

Margriete van Wijck and Jacobus van Vrederic,
having a personal moment in the kitchen.

The letter from Margriete had taken me back to the memory lanes of a love story I never thought I would share. It's a wound that was better left closed. If opened and unsealed, then I wondered how I would seal the open wound when the part I needed to seal it with was no more.

I didn't know if I would be able to tolerate the open wound that just opened on its own. I realized I needed to follow the dried tears to a magical well where I had left all my tears to the eyes of the beholder of these tears, my eternally beloved. It is she who would say these are my eyes but her tears.

A leap year had entered my life as I entered the 1st of January 1572. Many thought this year would be a very lucky year. As others thought, this would be a disastrous year as the war continued between the Dutch and the Spaniards. The resistance continued on the Dutch side. One good thing for the Dutch was the Spanish King Philip II did not like traveling so he actually avoided traveling to the Netherlands. Hopefully, this would give us an advantage by victory being on our side.

Treasonous conspirators of the war were being captured and severely punished by both sides. So, my noble merchant father had me placed inside of the stone fortress for months in fear I might end up supporting the wrong side of the war. Or maybe he did care somewhere inside of his stone fortress soul. Or maybe he was again concerned about his family honor if I were found to be supporting the wrong side.

My father on the other hand loved traveling, so I was always left behind with a house filled with staff who essentially brought me up. I had picked up character traits from my own household staff rather than my own blood, my father. I spoke different dialects spoken by the staff members. Life was not bad at all when my stone-hearted father was abroad.

Aunt Agatha was my household guardian. She was my nanny, my educator, and the person to go to for all of my needs. At the age of twenty, I had only one thought, a woman. I wanted to go out and search for the woman of my dreams, a special someone to spend the rest of my life with. Finally, like other young men, I could think of having a family of my own. I daydreamed of having a lot of children and I would be a loving, caring, fun father.

I was told about women whom I should pursue as a noble suitor. Yet I found no interest in any of the prospective women I was told to court. I felt like this society pushes you into a cage where you become a prisoner of their will.

The word suitor was in my eyes the wrong path, as where in this process was love involved? Where were the sleepless nights and daydreaming to be together forever? I had no one with whom I could share my thoughts, yet the pressure to find a woman and be her suitor was very strong from the unjust society. The same society that gave nothing to satisfy my want, however, pressured to take away my liberty.

I asked my only go-to person Aunt Agatha, "Aunt Agatha, may I ask you a question on love and women?"

She looked at me and just gazed at me, as I thought her glare kept going on for days or hours.

Aunt Agatha only said, "I am a Catholic nun, working in your home during a war. I really don't want to lose my job or my head."

She continued and said, "Life is a miracle. Take it as you go, and magical things will happen when you expect them the least."

I told her, "I don't want to be forced into pursuing a woman and becoming her suitor."

She only hugged me, whispered a prayer, and left. That night, I had found myself with a very high fever and a chill I thought I was dying from. The storm outside had the storm inside my body quiet for a while, until I started to moan in pain and was having hallucinations.

A young maiden came into my room and asked me if I was alright as there were no domestic helpers left for the night. I watched this angel from Heaven and thought she was the most beautiful woman on Earth sent down by God himself for me. She realized I was in some sort of discomfort as she never left the room. The next morning, I found her asleep next to me on a chair with a wet cloth in her hand.

She stayed awake all night changing cold compressions to reduce my fever. The stormy night had been a blur and I wished I could have remembered as this fair maiden was like an angel. I wondered if she was a new help or a distanced poor family member. She looked very different as her attire was different from all the women in town and my domestic helpers.

As the sun streamed inside, she jerked up and apologized for falling asleep. I wanted her to feel bad and somehow wanted her to never leave at the same time. I had this strange feeling toward her as if I had known her all of my life. Her hair was brown, and her eyes were like the ocean, deep yet brown. She was very petite and small but somehow very bubbly and alive. I wanted her to always stay around me with her everlasting bubbles of joy.

I asked her, "Who are you? What is your name? No one is allowed to enter my room or sleep on top of me without my permission!"

She replied, "I am an orphan, raised at the orphanage by the nuns of the Catholic Church. I came with Sister Agatha to give you all a helping hand. A lot of your domestic helpers have come down with the fever that is going around. So, your home needs an extra set of hands."

I was shocked no one had informed me that my household staffers had taken ill. A merchant friend of my father had traveled for days and had given my father's letter to a horseman who had then delivered a letter advising Father would be delayed due to a certain fever. Some of his merchant friends had fallen ill but were not too serious. I was used to living alone as my father would be missing for months at a time.

My thoughts were interrupted as she spoke again, "My name is Margriete van Wijck. I am of Dutch origin, but I was raised by nuns. I don't know how to cook or clean as I am training myself to become a wood merchant so I can help liberate my country. I will travel to Haarlem and fight with my countrymen against the Spanish invaders."

I was shocked at her words and her courage. She was lost in her own world.

She spoke again, "I don't like the war and the bloodbath, so I will help my countrymen in every way I can to stop this war. If I can't help stop this bloodbath, then I will become a Catholic nun and maybe help preach peace not war."

She asked me directly looking into my eyes with her big brown eyes, "What about you? You won't help in this war, or will you just sit home and hide in your richness?"

I was shocked at her words and courage, how a household help had spoken with her eyes looking straight at me, with her very small petite self, very stern in her position. I didn't know what about this woman stirred everything inside me, but I just wanted to hold on to the strong but soft woman. I knew she was afraid of life and knew how to fight and fend for herself. She was a very strong woman yet very soft in the inside.

I answered, "I don't believe in war. I find love much more attractive than war. I won't ever start a war, but since we are amidst a war, I will do my share to help my country. I will also help all innocent people; it matters not what side they are on. Life is precious and should never be taken as we can never return this back."

She asked, "So, you will never take what is not yours, right?"

I knew what she was saying in a strange way, yet I found her question strange as I was so attracted to her. I wanted to say, you I will have at any cost, even at my last breath. But I will make sure your last breath is taken after my last breath. I want to see you until my last breath.

I wondered if she could read my mind, as she only stared at me and said, "I am not scared of death. I am terrified to be left alone all by myself as this loneliness was a part of my unwanted gift from birth."

I told her, "Then you can give me the loneliness and have your wish of being free from ever being lonely. I don't mind the loneliness. I like the quiet nights and the even quieter days."

She watched me and said, “You don’t know how it feels to be loved and feel the blessings of a family. I have my church family and the everlasting love of the sisters in the church. I love being loved and giving love.”

I prayed for her as I told her, “May you find everlasting love and a person who loves you eternally even after his last breath.”

Time passed by as days went to weeks, as I had spent what seemed like eternal everlasting time with this very small, petite, and bubbly woman. On a very stormy and windy night, I had ended up in the church with her as I was begging the pastor to marry us in holy matrimony. We did not want to sin and we were both adults.

Somehow things had changed. We were back at my family’s carriage house on this very stormy night. The skies were pouring. The lightning bolts were displaying a lightshow. The drums were so hard we could hear nothing. We took our eternal wedding vows and consummated our marriage in the carriage house. By God, I had loved her on that night, I still love her today, and will forever love her eternally.

The best night in my life was very short-lived as my father had arrived and had sent my brave wife far away from me. I searched for her everywhere but could not find her. He spread rumors she had become a Catholic nun and was killed by the resistance fighters. My father's false rumors had separated my love from myself physically.

I, however, wondered if he knew he could never separate us spiritually. For within each breath of mine, she lives. The first night I saw a breadbasket filled with a crying child, I knew the love of my life never left me but had kept our love and proof of our union safely hidden from this world.

Why did you not share this secret with me Margriete? Did you not trust me? I knew my father must have told lies and blackmailed all to keep all of this hush. I searched everywhere yet she was so close to me, giving birth to our child all alone because society and social status holders make the rule of the class and order of a human.

I could still hear her words as she would sing to me, "I shall always be around you like a shadow, to protect you from all harm and evil of this cruel world, so help me God."

I had prayed may God keep you safe within his protection only for me. You were born for me and I was born for you and our child. I vowed I will find our child with my last breath and I will keep my promise as I was, am, and shall always be your true and only beloved. I will to the last breath only preach love and peace.

You were born and raised in a church, you married and gave birth in a church, and your last breath was taken in a church. So, for you, I had become a preacher of the church for you are my only and forever love. Eternally, I am yours.

Don't worry about me sweetheart, for I shall never be anyone else's. Forever, I am only yours and shall always be yours. As promised to you on a very stormy wedding night, I shall never let you go. Through my love, you shall always be mine.

I still remember her last words, like a windchime whispering in my ears, as she had touched my ears with her warm lips ever so gently and breathlessly said, "Jacobus, my love, I shall never let you go."

CHAPTER FOUR:

A FATHER'S LAST HOPE

"Hope glimmers through the dark nights as she converts herself to dawn, at times to find hope for others even at the cost of burning herself."

Jacobus van Vrederic and fisherman Altfrit van Visser, in Scheveningen, Den Haag during the fisherman's last moments.

ar broke through my land and bloodshed spread all over the country. Land and freedom come at a cost. Sometimes the cost is payable and at times the sacrifices are just sacrifices that can't be weighed by the scales of life.

My father's passing had left me free from any responsibilities or ties binding me to my home or town. I became a Protestant minister as I searched for my only child throughout land and water.

I kept my heart filled with the memories of my beloved, as I searched for our child. With my eyes, I searched for you, yet I knew you were watching through my eyes, Margriete. Within my hands, I always felt your hands.

Strange it may sound yet when I got tired and felt like I was about to fall, I somehow stood up as if you were holding on to me. I didn't see you, but you were there. I didn't hear you, but you talked nonstop. I walked with your given hope as I knew time was just my enemy.

Everyone I loved left me, yet time never did. I would search upon Earth and you would search in Heaven, and somehow God would guide us to her. In every lost and stranded child, I found our daughter. I tried to be there for the Catholics, Protestants, and all religious and non-religious children of God.

Bloodshed did not stop at Naarden as it spread throughout the land. I acquainted myself with a group of gypsies and traveled through the war-ridden cities. I entered Zutphen, Haarlem, Oudewater, and Maastricht. Mistrust and bloodshed from both sides spread throughout the land.

I had traveled to Alkmaar, Roermond and Gorcum where I found out Protestants and Catholics were both involved in bloodshed. I tried to see if my child was with the Catholics or the Protestants. I searched in all the churches I could get into. The Catholics and Protestants both were involved in the bloodshed and no sign of mercy from either side was given or asked for.

After searching for years, there were no signs of my child anywhere. Fear of being hunted down by either side was gripping the air. Time flew by very slowly, yet it did pass as neither did the war end nor my search. I finally caught up with the fisherman by the shore of the North Sea in Scheveningen.

The North Sea had greeted land here. This part of the country was more famous for being known as the fisherman's village. The fishermen would sail out to sea for days as their wives would wait for their return.

I too waited for the return of a certain fisherman no one knew of. After long days and even longer nights of waiting, I was taken to the hut of an injured fisherman. It was an old hut he lived within.

The huts all looked similar with a lot of fishing rods, fishing nets, and canoes for the fishermen to go sailing in. The fishermen would go sailing for days in a row. The wives would wait for their husband's safe return and I had waited with them as I worked as a Protestant preacher. The fishermen traveling through the rough sea even during a war, knew at all times their beloved family waited for their safe return with hope as their guide.

After such a long wait, I had finally entered the hut of the fisherman, I had ignored so many years ago. With all my courage rounded up, I entered his little hut. There, waiting for me was worse news. I found the wounded fisherman, Altfrit, taking his last breath. I sat next to him on a very old, soiled bed that smelled of fish and seawater.

I asked him, "Altfrit, don't leave me now. I have traveled throughout the country for my daughter. I realized too late as she is all I have left on this Earth. Please don't leave without guiding me to her. I need to hold her at least once. You were right. I need to see her at least once."

He smiled and held on to my hands as he said, "My dear nobleman, but you are too late. When the soldiers attacked, I sent my wife and our daughter, your child, to Amsterdam. I have not been able to get in touch with them yet. My wife and I have not had any child of our own as we have given all our love to our adopted child. Society has not been kind as our daughter is always teased as the illegitimate child of a nobleman."

I knew what he had meant. The world is a very unkind home for this world has people like me.

He then continued, "We gave her our love but from afar as even my wife had felt strange being a religious woman. Her birth mother had named her Griet van Jacobus. Kindly find her and let my family know I shall be the fisherman who will guide them like a lighthouse even from beyond."

Hands in my hands, he took his last breath. With his last breath, my hope found its last breath. The never-ending war had come to my land to free us from the Spaniards. Yet here I find no freedom from this bloodshed war. I had engaged myself in an interior war to find the last breath of hope left behind by my love.

I prayed for the very kind, short, and chubby fisherman. He always attired himself in typical overalls and always smelled like fish from the North Sea. Even on his deathbed, it was as if he was ready to go back to his favorite North Sea to fish.

The fisherman had not aged in the twenty years since the night he had entered my stone fortress and was ruthlessly sent away. The fisherman Altfrit had died by the North Sea. With my eyes closed, I could see him fishing happily in his final resting place, the North Sea.

I walked into church after church. Tired and frail, I yearned to go home, but where would I find a home when the people I had wanted to build a house with, were only a mist? The sandcastles being built on the sands had a family lovingly building them for a while. Still, I had no one even for a little while with whom I too could build a house on the sand until the seawater washes it away.

I enjoyed my sweet dreams of the freezing nights. As always, my beloved Margriete, came to visit me in my dreams. She would watch me in my sleep and even then, she would not say anything. I would wake up on top of wet pillows where the stains from the tears would be the only proof of yes, I too had loved a woman once upon a time.

Time had separated us my eternally beloved yet for me, time shall always belong in the past with you. You are my past and your love is my present. Your hope is the future I look upon. I yearned to be guided to our daughter, yet I only had my prayers to guide me.

I asked Altfrit, the fisherman, to guide me in my dreams, hoping he could somehow help from the beyond. As this world would not help a husband or a father, maybe the beyond would. I hoped for a miracle to guide me through this fog. My inner soul kept on hearing him repeat, “Are you sure you don’t even want to see her once?”

After searching for my daughter for nearly twenty years, in July of 1592, I met a young Catholic soldier by the name of Theunis Peters. He was fighting for the King of Spain. He had imprisoned me for fighting against the words of King Philip II and trying to help all the war victims I could, be the person a Protestant or a Catholic.

He asked me, “Are you not loyal to your King? Are you a resistance fighter who has gone against all the beliefs of the Spanish rulers?”

I told him my personal beliefs, "It is not that I am not loyal to the King, but I believe in freedom. I believe religion should be separate from state. People should have freedom of speech and have freedom to express individual religious values. Our society should be based on trade, ship builders, and fishermen, not only nobles."

I had to stop and take a break as I believed I lost Margriete and we were separated because of religious and social differences and hate.

I told him, "Everyone needs to have more tolerance. I don't support the oppression enforced on us by the King. I don't support the burning of churches or statues by the Protestants either. Even though I am a Protestant, I believe the love of my life and my only child might have been burned to death by the massive iconoclastic movements of the Calvinists. I believe as they burned down the statues and images of the Roman saints, they burned down the church my family had taken shelter within."

He said, "Freedom will be found but at what cost? It is hard for me too as I am only doing my job, but I too have a heart. How do I separate my personal feelings and my duty? You are the second prisoner of war I have whom I don't want to capture. I have another young maiden who reminds me of you. She is searching for her father, roaming around disguised as a nun."

Theunis continued, "You might be the person she is searching for. You might know her as she is the most mystically beautiful fair maiden this Earth has gifted. Her name is Griet van Jacobus, the only child of Jacobus van Vrederic."

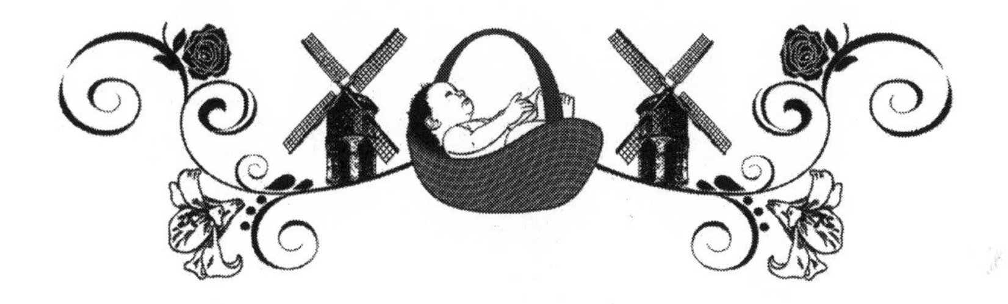

CHAPTER FIVE:

FORBIDDEN DAUGHTER

"Forbidden you are, then why does my heart say you belong to a father you don't know of, yet I know you are mine?"

Griet van Jacobus, searching for a father she never knew yet loved all her life.

Griet van Jacobus, my daughter, had found me. The joy of knowing she was out there somewhere removed all my sleep and worries. For nearly twenty years, I had searched land and shore for this child. Yet she had found me through the words of different churches. I thought a prayer does get answered even if it is twenty years late.

Pouring rain drenched the low-lying, flood-ravaged country. Maybe one day, the Dutch will befriend water and reclaim land from the ravaging seawater. Until then, we must be patient and hope the sea will be patient with us.

Patience had been the food of my soul. The burning pain of wanting to touch the one you love was so great, I didn't think I was a human. How could I keep all my feelings locked up in a cage? My solace was I was the unjust, who gave his word yet did not keep it. My lonely tears and screams of the dark nights were hidden within the walls of my empty nest and dark, arrogant pride.

Theunis asked, "You loved her a lot, your lover. You never married nor could you forget her. Then, why did you not accept her?"

I thought how much did he know? How did he know my life stories? How I longed to tell the world my Margriete was my eternally beloved wife. Yet what was the difference if I accepted her within my soul, or in a church, or on paper?

The hidden and secret love life of a nobleman, I could not speak of or share as Theunis spoke, "Yolente Visser-Wouter, an old fisherman's wife, had fresh baked bread, pickled herring, and soup for all the soldiers. She never asked which group of soldiers we were, Spaniards or the Dutch. We all honored her as a great woman. Some soldiers though are ruthless and have hunted down men, women, and children. I have been working for the King, but I have tried to save all the women and children. I have tried to hide them as much as possible. I could not save the fisherman's wife as she was caught in the middle of a crossfire."

I asked him fearfully, "You found my daughter? Is she alive? Is she okay?"

I waited for his reply. As he took so long to answer, I feared what could be wrong? Why was he not saying anything? He was oblivious to my questions as he only stared into blank space. Theunis started to breathe and sigh.

Then, he smiled and said, "Yes, I have found her, the love of my life. The breath of my existence. Musical harmony for my everlasting soul. Dawn appears when she awakens with a smile. Darkness evolves all around when she sleeps quietly."

I kept on bothering him for details and asked him to take me to her. I begged him to imprison me with her if we are both his enemy. He was still missing as if he was somewhere else. He had a blank stare on his face. I thought he was neither here nor there. I wondered was he in any sort of pain? Why did he look so pale?

I observed he was six feet tall with a very muscular body. The young soldier was in his twenties. His hair was long and blond, waving with the wind. His eyes were deep blue, and I knew he was of Dutch origin not from Spain, or maybe mixed.

I asked him, "What does she look like?"

His answers were a little shaky as if he was not stable. I watched his hands shake while his voice was shaking too. I thought why I never noticed these things before. I wanted to hold on to him selfishly as I wanted more information about my child.

The human mind sees what it wants to see. So, I saw a rough and tough soldier standing in front of me. I missed out on the very human standing in front of me.

Theunis kept on speaking, "Black hair, like a raven. Brown eyes, like Earth. Red lips like an apple. Olive-colored skin like a mystical fairy. Medium height of about five feet, five inches. She had the grace of a goddess. The heart was filled with love and laughter. The woman who looked like no one around her. She was very different. The everlasting beauty all painters want to paint and keep a portrait of. I keep her portraits in my eyes."

I knew he was describing my mother who was of Indian origin. My father had brought me back with him from India and never went back for his wife. He had worked for the Portuguese, as they had ruled India. My father was glad I did not turn out to be Indian looking. I never understood how he fell in love with an Indian yet did not have the courage to bring her back home. I guess it ran in the family.

The soldier spoke again, "Griet had said her mother knew she had some Indian blood, as the rumors were there, that her paternal grandmother was of Indian descent. Nonetheless, she also looks so much like you. She has your face and your looks but an Indian version of you. She has a famous name where she comes from. Everyone calls her, the mystical forbidden daughter."

I was shocked. Why forbidden? What do they mean my child is forbidden?

He replied without my asking, "Forbidden she was to enter her father's estate. Forbidden she was to enter any church as she was illegitimate. Forbidden she was to enter any school as she had no father's name. Her adopted parents tried to give her a name and a place, but they too were severely punished and thrown out for raising an illegitimate child."

Theunis stopped and went near the tent's opening. He held on to the tent for support. I assumed it was for mental support. Yet at hard observation, I worried if he was in any pain or discomfort. My thoughts, however, died at my lips. I could feel the pain of all others, but I couldn't express or show any.

He then continued, "They loved her and moved from place to place to keep her hidden from the cruel society who refuse to accept a forbidden daughter. All her life, she was called by children and adults as being the forbidden child."

I thought how I could do this when my child was not illegitimate? I had secretly married my wife and had this hidden from everyone in fear of societal backlash against her. The differences in our social backgrounds were created by the society because I let them as Margriete was my household help. If only I could have changed destiny.

My father never accepted this union. He called this union an illegitimate affair. My father had warned me he would not only ruin Margriete but also anyone who was related to her.

I never let her go as she was taken away from me with the grave trickery of a wealthy man. My own wealthy father had removed my wife and my child. I wondered if he worried what if my unborn child turned out to look Indian? Who would he have blamed for my daughter's beautiful looks?

I never let Margriete go. Even her last wish was to never let her go. We were separated by a ruthless soul and her last breath. But I never said anything as I knew he must have known all of this.

Theunis continued, "If you never accepted your beloved, then I wonder how could you allow society to come in between? Love is eternal and nothing can separate true lovers, not life nor death. No fear is greater than love, for where there is a competition between love and war, I know love will always be triumphant. I would not even allow death to invade my love story."

He stopped for a while and it was as if he was again lost in his own world. I let him gather his own thoughts. I wondered he would not let death come in between lovers, and I would not let death take my Margriete away from this Earth. So, I had kept her away from me.

Theunis then said, “If my love story ends with death, then I would cross the doors of life and unite with my beloved in death. I shall never let her go. The mystical forbidden daughter of this world, Griet van Jacobus, is forever my eternally beloved. Her only wish in life was to never let her go.”

I knew of another woman who too wanted me to never let her go. I did let her go as her last breath separated us. I hoped for my life that I would never let go of her daughter if I could win in the battle of life and death.

I wanted to let you know, my only child, my daughter Griet, you are my beloved daughter. How did you find your father who could not find you, even after a twenty-year journey? This father never let go of your mother, but she was taken away from me.

I would hold on to the last drop of hope without complaining about life or the unjust life has gifted me with. I only hoped one day I too would have someone who I could leave behind my life diaries with. Maybe she would share with this world the truth of a father's journey through love and war.

Today, I only wished I could find out how you found me as then I would let you know you are my beloved daughter, even though this unjust world called you the forbidden daughter.

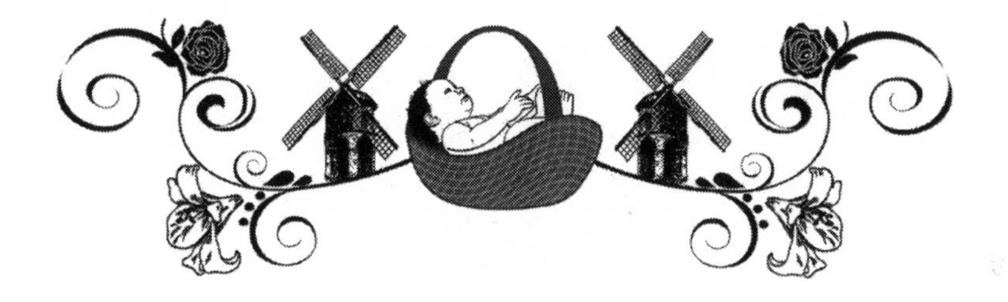

CHAPTER SIX:

FALLING IN LOVE

"Love lives on through the union of true lovers, beyond life and death."

Griet van Jacobus finds her beloved twin flame in Theunis Peters, as she delivers bread to him and his soldiers.

Heaven was pouring open all of her tears. This night, she stormed her sorrows and anger upon the land below. I watched nature and thought how this young man never worried.

All the soldiers outside our tent were worried and were thinking of moving out to a higher ground. The group of soldiers had no other prisoners outside of myself. I wondered why this bothered me.

I was traveling for years searching for a child I never knew. I realized I searched for a small breadbasket with a newborn child. I never realized my newborn had become a grown-up woman.

What if I had crossed her path and never realized? I prayed may I be able to see her at least once before my time on Earth is over. I would never again refuse a breadbasket, whether it has a child or bread, for a gift from God comes in different forms.

Theunis talked aloud, "Don't fear the heavens above, for I only fear the Earth below. Being left down here all alone scares me. To even think of being separated from my beloved is my nightmare. I would give up anything on Earth or even in Heaven above to be united with her. I fear leaving anyone or anything alone here on Earth."

I thought why he always talked about being left alone, for he had a long life ahead. Yes, this war had left all without any dream or hope but may my prayers be with him. It mattered not what happened to me, as long as he found complete love and happiness within his love and life.

Theunis smiled at me and started to talk, "I will only accept prayers to be united with my beloved in life or in death. So, you need to know I am not here to capture you, but to actually accompany you to your child or take her back home to your family home. She has yearned to be with you in your home at least for a day. My thoughts were maybe I could bring her to your family home in Naarden. I can't bear to be separated from her for too long, but I am here at her request. She has a special gift for you. She has been saving this gift and wanted to give it to you with her own hands."

I thought why he was keeping all this suspense and not telling me where my daughter was. What gift was he talking about? I knew I had no right asking about her, but I had devoted my life searching for her and he found me so easily.

I asked him, "How did you find me and where is my daughter? How did you fall in love with my child? I need to find the answers to all my unanswered questions."

He said nothing for a long time. We both heard the musical sounds of nature as I watched tears roll from the eyes of a very rough and tough soldier.

He abruptly started to talk, "The answers to your questions involve a very heart-rending love story. I hope you have time. Within this storm, we are going nowhere. I must travel separately in the morning. I will have you travel to Naarden with my group of soldiers. From Amsterdam, you can be there shortly as I will come to your family home with Griet shortly afterward. I must go to Steenwijk and get her from there. Oh, and I found you as you had left a trail to yourself by searching for your daughter. A father's quest had painted an easy road for the daughter to find her father."

I wondered what my daughter was doing there. I knew the Siege of Steenwijk had a bloody war. The Dutch Republic's army under Maurits van Oranje had two main transport roads blocked off. The Spanish troops just surrendered this July of 1592. The unsettled fights were still going on. I wondered why Theunis was trying to go back to a place his troops lost.

He spoke, "Yes, I was working for the King of Spain as that was my job. I found and was to capture your daughter as she was working with the Dutch under Maurits van Oranje. We had captured a lot of prisoners as the fisherman's wife Yolente and her adopted child were baking bread and fish for all the soldiers. They did not care who they attended to. As long as they could save a life, they would give a helping hand. My three-year love story began as a young woman brought me a basket of bread."

I thought the irony of this was this same woman was brought to me in a basket like bread. He walked up to the entry of the tent and took a deep breath. I never bothered him and did not want to interrupt his thoughts, so I remained quiet.

"A three-year love story between enemy forces started off abruptly as I saved a young woman from falling under the bullet fires from my own teammates. She smiled and said the two women are here to offer food as they knew we had none. Every night and every morning, these two women would arrive, and we talked for hours. Our conversations led to an eternal love story that pulled two souls into one as I could not control myself from being with her. Being near her, I watched how she would just dance in the rain like an angel. She would sit under the birch tree talking to her birth mother as if her mother was there in front of her."

I wanted to hear more about Margriete but I had no courage to say anything. I watched the young man, and his tears fall like a waterfall.

After a break, he started to talk again, "I fell madly in love with a woman from my enemy camp. She told me she does not believe in wars as she will preach love and spread only love. Like an angel, she walked into my life. The glowing moon's glory had flooded her aura. When she crossed the lake to come to our camp, the lake felt ashamed by her beauty. A shadow of love she was, always walking behind me, in front of me, and around me. For three years, we traveled together."

It was a dark day as the storms of the night kept getting louder, yet this soldier noticed nothing. I said nothing as the silence around us talked in volumes. I wondered where he was going and why was he lost in his world. I knew not to bother a sleeping dreamer as it can be dangerous.

He started to talk again, "We got married in the same church her mother had married secretly. The same Catholic pastor married us, and he wished for us to have a better end than the finale her mother had. We traveled together through a war-ravaged land where bloodshed and miseries flooded the land. I felt I was in Heaven as I was within the embrace of my beloved."

He stood up and was in his own world as he was thinking what he should say, or I thought he was thinking what not to say.

He continued, "On a very stormy night, Griet came from nowhere. I walked behind her as she was floating on the water. I asked her what is it my love, why are you here? I was in a war tent where bloodshed had been the only path. She was in a church. Griet was not well due to some physical illness. She started to run as I ran after her. I found her in an invisible form like a cloud as she led me to a body shot near the lake."

He stopped and made a fist with his hand. I just watched him and waited for him to talk.

Then, he said, "I could not understand what was going on. My Griet watched me as she tried to wipe off my tears. Her shot body moved very slowly. She spoke very softly as she gave me this diary of hers. This diary never said, 'Dear Diary' but it read, 'Dear Papa.' I watched the love of my life slip away as she was shot by my own group of soldiers by accident, mercilessly. She smiled and told me not to cry but kiss her one last time."

Theunis stopped talking and I realized he was reliving the worst part of his life all over again.

He continued, "She said she had found the sweet kisses of her husband on her lips but missed being a child of a father or a mother. No father gave her a fatherly kiss, no mother hugged her and kissed her goodnight. Her adopted parents never touched her even though they brought her up."

Theunis placed a hand in his hair as if he was here but not here at all. He said, "They always told her she was an illegitimate child. The world called her the forbidden daughter. I held her in my chest and gave her a lover's last kiss. I told her to never say goodbye as I will travel through life and death to be with her."

He stopped for a while as he spoke again, "Griet asked me to make a promise. I will deliver the diary and her special gift to you. She searched for you everywhere. It was as if you were always a step ahead of her. She knew you were searching for her as we both ended up where you had left. I will keep my promise and give you her last gift."

The storm outside intensified with lightning and thunder as we both watched the musical concert of the night. He raised his voice so I could hear him over the sounds of the storm outside. Yet no one could have stopped the storms inside my inner soul.

He said, "A promise from a beloved was made that night. From my soul was a promise made to my beloved. I wondered why she was shot on the back. Her spirit whispered in my ears, that it is because everyone in her life had betrayed her from the back. Even life betrayed her at her last breath. I held on to her as we were separated by a breath. I wanted her to breathe in my mouth as I could catch on to her last breath. With our final kiss as my lips were on her lips, it is then I promised her, this beloved is and shall always be your true eternally beloved."

He stopped as he was trying to control his inner pain. I watched him as he said, "Her adopted mother Yolente was shot as well. They both got shot by the people they brought food to. The fisherman's wife wanted to be with her husband near Scheveningen, so I had arranged her body to be sent over there."

If only I could have seen her a few days ago. Our paths must have crossed yet we missed one another. I heard everything and knew my life again just died in front of me. I asked my Creator how many times he would watch me die before my punishment ends.

I watched the young soldier leave a diary on the table. On the front of the diary, it said, "Dear Papa." He also had a note which said, "Don't open the diary until you get your next gift. Your gift shall be waiting for you at your family home in Naarden."

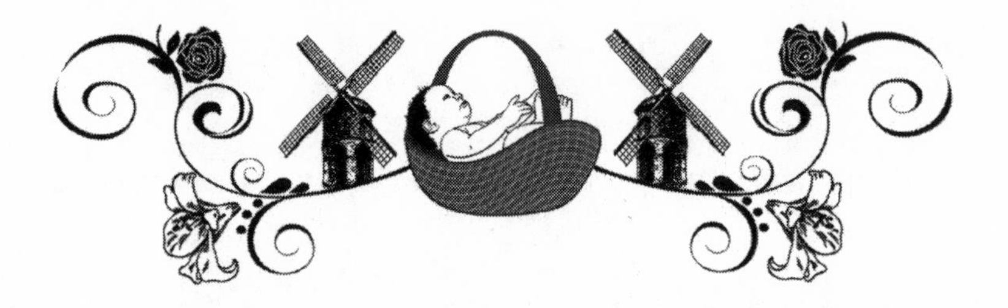

CHAPTER SEVEN:

SOLDIER'S HONOR

"Taking an oath from the mouth is just an oath, yet a soldier taking an oath to unite with his beloved even tearing Earth and Heaven apart is a soldier's honor."

Jacobus van Vrederic and Theunis Peters, having a private talk in the soldier's tent.

The moon outside had suddenly wanted to glow upon the Earth. She removed all the clouds and whispered to all, tonight let there be peace. Let this night be a night of recollection through memory lanes of life. May the saddest songs on Earth be embarrassed at the tearful path of my life.

The ocean in my eyes had dried up. There was not even a drop of tear remaining within my tear well. I had seen statues of great men standing upon Earth. Today, I saw the reflection of a real stone statue in the reflecting waters of life as I viewed my self-reflection.

I looked upon the skies as I screamed in my head, "How could I have tears left Margriete? Answer me! Did you not say your tears, my eyes? You left with all of my tears and now you have taken my child too. I need someone to hold on to. I need my child. I want to raise her, but how?"

I had to control myself and give all my strength to a young soldier. I watched the young soldier prepare for his journey back to Steenwijk. I admired his willpower and determination. I just wished he could have given me some advice as to how I should go on without anything to hold on to.

Yet I held all my emotions within my stone wall, so I could be of help to this young soldier and not be an obstacle. He watched the moon as he laughed to himself.

He said, "Griet loved the full moon sparkling in the water. She wished she could hug the moon but knew maybe the moon is shy like her and avoids any hug. She would swim in the lake and try to hug the moon's reflection. I must return to my beloved quickly, so I can deliver her to you. She is waiting all alone for you. She needs you to hold on to through life."

I asked him, "How would you do that? Has she not been buried yet? How do you want me to hold on to someone who has left me before our union? If only I had another chance, if I could go back in time, I would have changed so many things. But how do I hold on to someone God too wants for himself?"

He watched me with a shock in his eyes and stood up in a confrontation sort of way. He shook himself to settle his nerves and did not speak for a while.

Then, he asked me, "You wanted her to be buried in an unknown spot, like a dead person? This is Griet, my beloved. I have kept her body in a coffin box, all ready to travel back home, to her father's home."

I watched him and replied, “I would travel to the end of this Earth to have my daughter back home with me. But how will you do it? Does the body not deteriorate with time?”

He got mad and started to walk back and forth as he replied in a very deep voice, “No, it shall not, as it is not a body but my beloved. She did not die but is just a breath away. She made her promise. She will wait for me as I promised we shall forever be together, in life or death. She is a miracle. Even the Catholic pastor and the Protestant minister both have told me she is a miracle. All have agreed she is asleep, and nothing can harm her body. Even though this world never loved her, God did. I believe God created her for me and me for her. We shall be together throughout eternity.”

He stopped himself abruptly as he needed air or something to breathe. He made groaning sounds as he watched the heavens above and cried and said, “Dear God, up there, please allow my beloved to await me. I wanted to give her a final name. She was not allowed to return to her father’s home alive, but no one said she can’t return dead. I also want to deliver her last gift safely to her father. Please gift me the gift of time, so I may complete the honorable job of a husband and keep a wife's last wish."

I watched him and knew there shall be a miracle as I have heard of a lot of stories of bodies not deteriorating at all, like miracles from beyond. I wondered if God had listened to my final prayers and had kept her alive even in death for me. I knew I was the biggest sinner left alive on Earth, still I hoped my prayers would be answered by my Creator.

I only prayed for a man who was praying for his beloved and not for himself. I prayed may all my prayers be given to this young man and may his prayers be answered. As a preacher, I had prayed for so many along my journey, within so many different churches. Today, however, I only prayed for a stranger I called my son.

Theunis asked, "Will you honor her and allow me to bring her back to your home which you could accept as her home? Her last wish was to unite with you. So, I would ask you to honor her last wish. Please accept her gift and her."

I was shocked at his request and told him, "She is the child I always wanted yet never had as I am the father who sent her away. If I could gift her all my life only to see her at least once, I would. I am the father who has not even seen his daughter once. Don't ask me why I feel this way, but I only have you who links me to her, so I really don't want to lose you too. My prayers are may all your wishes come true. Maybe this is a father's worry, but what about your parents or family?"

He only watched me as he told me, "My parents were both killed by the Dutch Republic's army. This is what war does to everyone. A war sees nothing, hears nothing, and spares nothing, then I ask how is a war fair? I am Dutch as my father was fighting with the Dutch. My mother and her family were fighting with the Spaniards. My parents separated because of the war. I found the love of my life because of the same war, in an enemy camp."

I told him, "To free a country and the future generations, we are all sacrificing our lives and loved ones. No words can justify this to our minds except we must walk with life and let this tear-filled journey end as we wipe off the tears of others at any cost."

I wanted to give him a hug, but I knew real men don't hug or cry or show emotions. I was scared to bring him closer to me because when I start to bring people closer to me, they leave me and go to a place I can't bring them back from. So,

I just stood there lost in my own thoughts. He watched me, came closer, and hugged me tight.

He said, "I don't know why but it felt right. I know I would have wanted to hug and hold on to Griet as much as I could, if only she were forever mine. Do remember to hug all who mean something to you. You don't want to wait until tomorrow for tomorrow is not known."

I never said a word as I too knew it felt right, but how come I never do what feels right and always live to regret?

He then told me, "I will be away for a while as I shall bring her home. I want your promise that you will honor her by adding a tombstone that says 'Griet van Jacobus, the beloved daughter of Jacobus van Vrederic and Margriete van Wijck.' This way she would get recognition and unite her parents through name, if not through life then at death."

For the first time in years, tears rolled out of my eyes as I replied to him, "Even with the last breath in my life, I will keep my promise and have it done. A father's promise. But this old father wishes to be your companion on the journey back to get my child. It was I, who had sent her away, so it is I who wants to bring her back home through her last journey. I also want you to place a sign on the same tombstone saying beloved wife of Theunis Peters."

He just smiled and I knew he just finished his part of the promise made to his beloved.

He only said, "You may accompany me as I have arranged for both of our travel gears. We shall bring her home. This is a soldier's honor. For your prayers given to me, I accept them to be with Griet forever, not if she was mine, but I will always be hers. You may place my name on her tombstone, how you choose to do so. I have complete faith in you and your words."

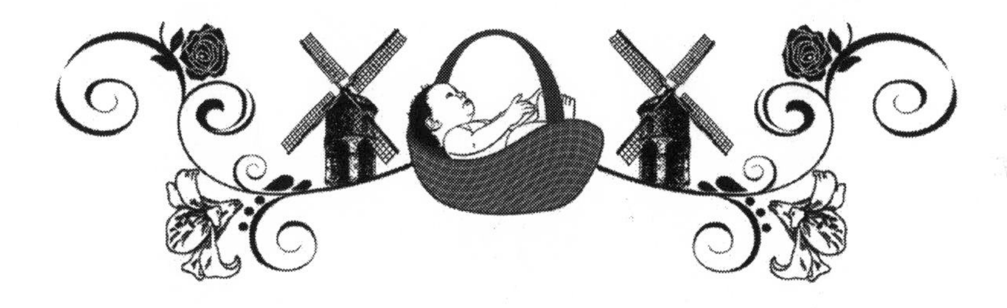

CHAPTER EIGHT:

THE COFFIN

"Life ends as the last breath is taken, yet a lover's memory keeps the beloved alive even within a coffin."

Theunis Peters, hovering over the coffin covering the view from Jacobus van Vrederic.

A country was under siege as two sides fought a fierce battle. Steenwijk had been under attack and the roads were damaged through failed and successful bombardments from both groups. Mines were detonated under bastions during the attack on the 5th of July 1592.

Days had passed by as Theunis had traveled to me and now we were traveling back. We had to travel days to be near Steenwijk. It was a very hard journey as all the roads had been severely damaged. Enemies were looming all around even though this part was liberated.

We had traveled through land and water for days as Theunis had people helping us. The Spanish troops had lost Steenwijk as they gave the city over to the Dutch and English troops. This made the return journey easier even though there were soldiers all around who were still fighting one another.

I watched a young lover and his determination to bring his beloved back home. He had my admiration within true love flourish. I believed then, what was death as even after death this young man lives for his beloved.

After going around for days to get people off our track, we arrived in Giethoorn, a place that looked like paradise for lovers. I was glad my child passed away here within the embrace of her beloved. I worried though how we would take my daughter's coffin out of here without letting anyone see us. To enter or exit Giethoorn, one must use a boat.

He knew what I was thinking as he answered my question, "With love and care, we shall take this coffin back home."

He took me to a secret cave hidden under the heavy bushes of flowers. There were water lilies spread all over this town. I knew the artist, the majestic Creator, had given my daughter a sacred place to say her final farewell.

I heard there was screaming in the background. I jumped up in fear for a young man I considered my son.

He came in and told me in a whisper, "We must keep quiet until dark. Then, we will walk by foot, travel by boat, and then by carriage to carry the coffin back home."

I watched the lover take a mahogany wood coffin that looked like a double coffin out from under the bushes. He kissed on top of the box ever so lightly. He touched the box and hugged it as he said, "Sweetheart, your beloved is back. A beloved has promised his beloved, I shall never let you go."

He then held on to it as he laid his head on top of it. He told me, "We won't open it until it reaches the destination, so we could give her some respect and privacy."

I knew it was to preserve the body. Through the glass top, one could view the body, but he placed his head on top of it covering the view for everyone else. I never asked to see her as I knew then I would not be able to complete my journey back home and keep my given word to an honorable soldier.

The fight outside in the open air got worse as it got darker. I knew we had a war in our hands as the coffin was property of the army that shot her to die in the lake near Giethoorn. I wondered how a person could be even more ruthless than myself.

How could people shoot an innocent girl who gave them bread? I fought with emotions as I saw the breadbasket she had brought bread for the soldiers in was left behind. My daughter was brought to me in a breadbasket. If only I had accepted her then, today she would not have lost her life to yet another breadbasket.

I watched Theunis had taken out some golden guilders and gave them to a stranger. Then, we were given permission to take the coffin in peace. At all times, Theunis carried the breadbasket. He had allowed his group of confidantes to carry the basket and a few other things he wanted to keep with the coffin.

The journey home to Naarden was treacherous as even Mother Nature was against us. I sat in a carriage by myself as Theunis walked all along the way with the coffin. Never did he leave the coffin alone for he thought she would be scared amongst all of these soldiers.

He kept on speaking to her, “Sweetheart, we are almost home and then we will rest in peace. I shall never let you go, I promise. Hold on to me and you too never let me go. I want the final kiss from you before I fall asleep next to you. I will remember to hold on to you in a big hug as you were never hugged by anyone else because they all knew I am a very jealous lover.”

He kept on repeating, “I have your love and my love joined in a bundle of sacred blessings to keep me going.”

He sang sweet songs to her all along the way. The journey was hard and risky through the dark nights. We always traveled through the nights and rested during the days. Yet Theunis never closed his eyes in fear if he loses the coffin. I asked him to rest for a while, and I could be the watchman for him.

He smiled and said, “I can’t close my eyes for I fear what if I can’t open them again. May God give me enough strength, so I can take my beloved back home.”

We arrived in Naarden as the gates opened to a huge cold stone fortress. A huge circular brick paved driveway welcomed us through the prison like iron gates. In the middle was a bigger than life, old stone waterfall. I was the lonely landowner of this huge castle which was covered with overgrown vines.

The huge castle watched everyone who entered, warning all she is a lonely fortress. It was such a huge home, but it felt so lonely and cold. I thought nothing about the house pulls me to her, except the memories of my Margriete.

A typical Dutch gable roof covered the castle. The gray stone had aged and looked even more mystical in the dark. The rough stone castle looked like she never had a woman around to tend her in a motherly way. If you had entered this cold building, it smelled like men and men’s alcohol solution which men use to smell better. No children or their laughter could be heard. I only remember a child was brought here in a breadbasket who could not even enter this cold castle.

Nonetheless, it felt like drunk men. The mansion had the strict hard touches of a very arrogant man. At the back of the fortress was the carriage house, where I had asked my daughter's coffin box to be placed with honor and dignity as there were so many memories buried in the carriage house. I could still smell the wonderful, sweet memories of my Margriete.

I watched everyone who came with us take down the coffin box with love and tender. Theunis never let go of the box his beloved had laid within and I guess her breadbasket. His way of handling the coffin box would make all think my daughter was still alive within the box. I wanted to think she would jump up and say she is finally home.

Then, I remembered the words of a heartless man who had said my child should never enter this home alive. I watched the heavens above and thought, alive or dead, this is her home, and she will enter her home. If only I had the courage to utter the words to a heartless man. I wished I could go up to the skies and ask why I had no courage to walk out with my Margriete or my Griet. I wished I could take the days back and say no, to my own fate. I couldn't so I would do my part and welcome my child back home.

The caretakers of my home came and greeted us. The butler Bertelmeeus van der Berg came and asked,

"My Lord, you have finally returned home. You have come from abroad as you have a lot of things with you. What have you brought with you? Do we need more help? I can arrange for the men to come in the morning. I will get the house and guesthouse ready. I have shown all the people their respective rooms."

He was really happy even though this was the saddest day of my life. He then very strangely asked, "Do you need a nanny?"

I told him, "I have brought my daughter back home with me. I don't need a nanny as where she is, no nanny is needed."

He said, "I shall arrange a room for her, sir."

I kept my voice calm and did not break down or show my emotions to anyone. Never did I show any emotions to any household member of this house. The only one I did fall with, I was forbidden to love. Now my daughter too had landed upon the name forbidden daughter.

I hid my emotions in my own coffin of a heart as I replied, “No need for that as she will be resting in her own bed that came along with her. It’s the coffin.”

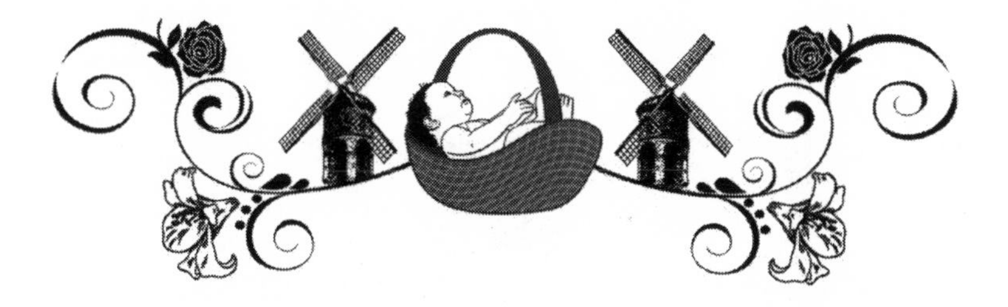

CHAPTER NINE:

NEVER LET YOU GO

"Love unites two minds, bodies, and souls into one. So, how could death separate these when they are inseparable?"

The carriage house decorated with flowers and candles, where a beloved child was conceived and bids her final farewell as she is a breath away.

All were quiet and nothing could be heard. There was no storm brewing outside. The huge stone castle stood as cold as ever. All the barn animals remained quiet and no carriages could be heard from near or afar. The night owls could not be heard. The singing lovebirds, the nightingales, too were quiet out of respect as today true twin flames, a beloved couple again united in a nearby carriage house.

Today, a daughter came home to her father as should all children after birth. Yet this lonely father brought his beloved daughter home at her death. I searched for you all your life, yet you hid away from me so to keep the words of your unkind grandfather. You avoided Papa's house during your little life, but you have come to bid your farewell to this heartless Papa.

Why did death hurt so much? My whole home was in a celebration mood as a daughter had returned home. My staff were all dancing with joy as a daughter had returned. But this celebration was blessed with tears, not laughter. I wanted to see my child, yet I had not, so I could give some privacy to her beloved grieving twin flame.

The majestical coffin box laid in the same carriage house, where I had made love to my twin flame, my beloved

Margriete. That's when and where my child was conceived. Today at the same sacred spot, my child laid asleep. I would visit her as soon as her beloved gave me a chance. I wanted him to take all the time he needed before the final farewell.

My thoughts were interrupted by the caretaker Bertelmeeus, "Sir, you should go to the carriage house and check on the young man. He was repeating the same phrase until he became very quiet. He neither is crying nor is he moving. He has been laying inside the same box."

I was not sure what this old man was saying as I never understood him anyway. He talked ever so quietly as if we were in a library. Each word was separated by a few seconds. I knew he had been there to raise me with Aunt Agatha. He was very close to Margriete and knew all of the family secrets.

Bertelmeeus was the only staff member who never left this home. Even without pay, he still resided here. His feelings he kept within himself. I must have picked up some of his character traits. Actually, he was the father I never had.

I got up and told him, "I will go as soon as the young man comes out of the room. I just want them to be alone for a while."

He repeated, "They will be alone and together for a long time, sir. He has been repeating the same phrase, Madam Margriete used to say."

I was shocked at his words. How did he remember what I had tried to forget? I did not want to ask him anything but knew I must go and visit my daughter. I wondered if the young man would allow me to see her.

Bertelmeeus was scaring everyone with fearful stares as if he saw a ghost. He also made his regular cold and fearful words and sounds. I avoided him and I walked over trying not to intrude into my daughter and Theunis's privacy. Yet the gripping silence also got chills in my soul. I prayed Theunis was well and able to handle the separation.

I called his name, "Theunis, may I come in please. I would like to bid my farewell to Griet before morning."

No one replied, so I entered the room filled with flowers. Lilies and roses were spread all over the room as were candles. The room smelled like flower fields from heavens above. The dimly lit candles gave them privacy of a romantic wedding night.

The room felt like a blessed wedding room and was full of love and tender. I could not see anyone there as the coffin box was closed. I went closer to the coffin box and realized it seemed like a twin box. I wondered why this never bothered me before but bothered me now. Why was there a twin coffin box?

During the journey, I had asked why the coffin box looked bigger than normal. I never got any answer, so I assumed it was to hide things in. I feared the worst as I found a note next to the coffin.

It was addressed to me and the letter read,

29th of July 1592

Dear Jacobus van Vrederic,

I hope you have rested well and are at peace to have your daughter finally home. I have kept my given promise and have brought her home to you.

I also have kept my given promise to my beloved and will not let her be alone.

No, I have not committed suicide or any such sort, but I too was shot as I tried to rescue my beloved and our sacred gift that will be delivered to you soon.

The gift is in the basket I carried along the way. I am positive you have noticed. The wound I suffered was quite serious, and I knew my time was limited.

I asked the Creator to give me enough time to bring a daughter back home to her father. My prayers were answered as I finally am able to sleep next to my beloved.

Her final words were to give her one last kiss and hold on to her as she is afraid of the dark. I promised her I will hold on to her.

I asked her to go to sleep and I will be by her side. Please keep us together in union throughout time in this joint coffin box.

My words be sealed with a kiss from a beloved to a beloved I had promised. Please know Griet is, was, and shall forever be my love, my life, my eternally beloved.

To her I had promised that even in death, we shall not be separated. A promise I shall keep throughout time, for I shall never let her go.

Yours Truly,

Theunis Peters

P.S. Your gift is in the basket and shall arrive to you shortly.

I finally got to see my child and her true beloved. My mystical beauty was sleeping peacefully. I touched her skin and it still felt warm to my touch. The exotic Indian beauty with her dark black hair, her olive-colored skin, and ruby red lips which had a smile on her face.

She was wearing all white, dressed like a bride. On her hands, she had white lilies. On her feet, rose petals were laid ever so gently. Theunis was attired like a groom. He had a smile on his lips as in ever after yours. I laid roses and lilies on both of them.

I saw he had space to hold on to her hands as he laid asleep. The coffin box closed on top of them, yet one could see the hands holding on to one another. Forever, Theunis had succumbed to his injuries which he had hidden very well from me. Again, I felt lonely and knew God never gives more pain than what one can take, so I really must be a human cut out from a rock or a stone.

I knew I must live to give these twin flames a place in history. The pages of history that shall fly away like the ever-moving clouds will retell the love story of a beloved forbidden daughter and her beloved. Yet if I could only spread the words of love and its true meaning then I must write within the pages of my diary, a father's love letter to his daughter and her beloved. Words failed me as I tried to utter them, yet words shall find a place within the pages of my diary through my pen and paper.

My words were never uttered to you my sweet child as they were always one breath away. I only wish this life would have allowed me to hold you at least once, in my arms. If I could feel your warm breath once, yet forever we are separated by a breath.

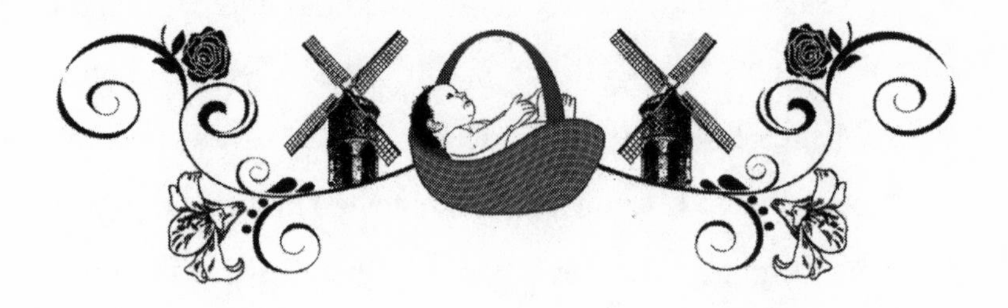

CHAPTER TEN:

A GIFT FOR GRANDFATHER

"The river of life gives and takes throughout time. We all stand by her shore to receive one more miracle as the waves pass by."

Butler Bertelmeeus van der Berg holding on to baby Margriete repeats, "I shall never let you go" as Grandfather Jacobus van Vrederic watches over.

Life was a strange journey where I found everything lost and never found. How would I go on without any hope? The frightful storm was quiet tonight. The pouring rain also gave me peace and quiet as she stopped dripping. Had heavens above dried up as you my dear Margriete took tears away from heavens above too? I wondered where Mother Earth's fearless storms had hidden.

I would control my own feelings for tonight I had guests whom I wanted to be permanent members of my household, yet they could only stay for a night. I would with all my love honor your last wish and keep you both united together throughout time. I wondered what gift my daughter had left behind. I would read her diary as promised after the burial.

Again, Bertelmeeus came and was shaking like his unusual self. He was smiling and laughing like he got a promotion or something. I wondered was he quitting after all of these years?

He said, "Sir, there is someone waiting outside for you. He has a basket with him. I wanted to ask you to at least take a look into the basket before you send it away. The person said the basket and the things inside are personal gifts from Griet van Jacobus and Theunis Peters."

I was shocked how much of a stone-hearted person do these people think I am? I would never again refuse a gift. The fear that had me refuse the last gift was because I wanted the child to live. I had my child back home with me, but I could not even feel her last breath. I told him to show the person in.

There in front of me was a soldier who had accompanied my child and her husband. He had a basket in his hands. I knew this was the same basket Theunis had carried along the journey. I was so scared as to what my child was holding on to as she took her last breath. She had provided bread to all the soldiers even to her deathbed.

The soldier spoke, "Sir, my last job before we head back out again, is to make sure you receive this basket. This was your daughter's last wish. She asked me to tell you to never let go of this gift."

He laid a basket in front of me, which moved as he moved away. I worried what was inside that moves. I watched Bertelmeeus was jumping up and down with joy as he had something in his hands. I avoided his eye contact as I took the basket in my hands.

There in the basket was a newborn baby, a few weeks old. She had a note in her basket with her. She opened her eyes and smiled. It felt so good as if my whole life just stood still. I wondered did I go back in time? Had my child been returned to me? Was it not years but days that had passed? I saw tears flooded my eyes as I heard a little baby sound alerting me of her arrival.

Bertelmeeus could not take the silence as he asked, “Sir, what does the note say?”

I saw there on a paper was clear handwriting from my daughter which read, a gift for Grandfather. I read the letter out loud,

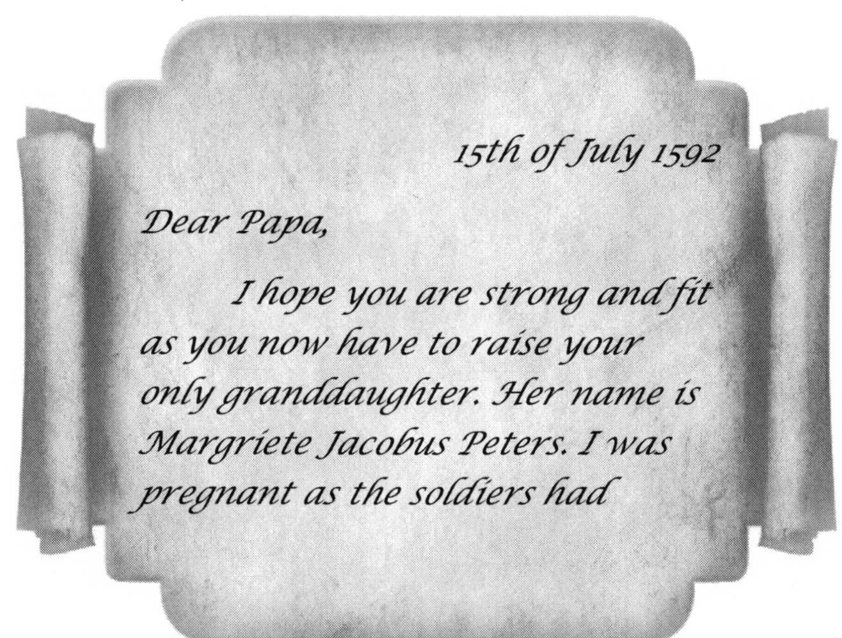

15th of July 1592

Dear Papa,

I hope you are strong and fit as you now have to raise your only granddaughter. Her name is Margriete Jacobus Peters. I was pregnant as the soldiers had *attacked and shot me. Yet Papa, I was a very strong child just like you.*

I fought to give birth to my daughter. I waited until Theunis had come back and had taken her to safety. I know Theunis too got shot as he was trying to take our daughter to safety.

Life has blessed me with a gift I can now pass on to my own father. The life I wanted from you, now my little girl can have with you.

I was told by the nuns who helped Mama give birth to me, my baby looks just like Mama. They came along all the way from Naarden to help with her birth too.

They promised they will with the help of Dutch and Spanish soldiers try to deliver my gift, your granddaughter, to you. I hope they or Theunis have found you.

Papa, I realized a war divides a country, yet a newborn child has united soldiers who had started the bloodshed. One of them told me he never meant to shoot me. He and his men shot a few people thinking they were all from the opposing side.

Yet both sides had regretted when they found out I was shot as well as my adopted mother. They have promised to do their share and make this right from their side.

I know my Papa is a preacher who has taught to forgive all. My Mama's message to me was to forgive and live.

So, as I have forgiven the soldier, I pray you too shall forgive my grandfather as today you too are a grandfather.

Papa, I pray you will hold on to her as your beloved, for I know she will never let you go.

Yours Truly,

Griet van Jacobus

I read the letter out loud as I saw Bertelmeeus pick up the young child. He said, "This great-uncle of yours will never let you go."

I told him to give me the baby. As I held on to her, I told her, "My child, mark of my eternally beloved, I shall never let you go."

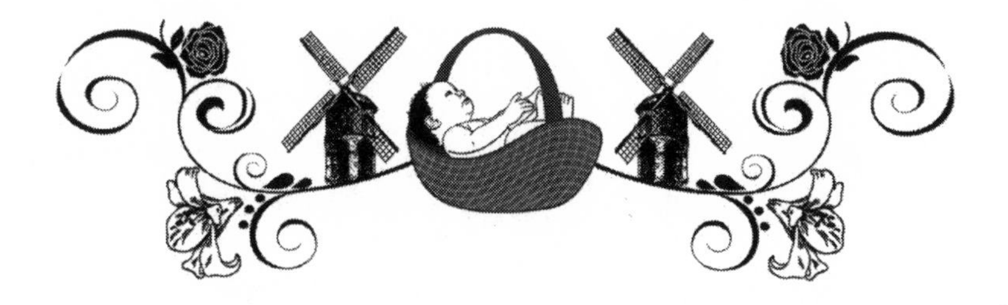

CONCLUSION:

EVERMORE BELOVED

"Life is a long journey yet here at all times do remember we are all separated by a breath."

A grandfather and his beloved granddaughter's journey together as they repeat, "I shall never let you go."

As I had asked in the beginning, why does Mother Nature show her fury, her anger, and her tears to all of us? I found the answer to my own question as I have learned it is better to show the anger, the fury, and the tears rather than burying them alive. I was never able to show any emotion, even though I felt all of the emotions this Earth bestows upon a human.

Yet today as I raise my granddaughter, we never forget to show any emotions. Every day, we repeat to one another, "I shall never let you go." I have brought my granddaughter, a two-year-old, to a very sacred garden. We come here often as this place renews our faith in true love. My adorable grandchild even at a very young age knows how to utter the words, "I love you." She knows love is eternal and shall only grow evermore throughout time.

I want all of you to come and visit a magical memorial garden. The garden is called *EVERMORE BELOVED*. This is a memorial paradise for a couple in a twin magical ever after grave. They are buried together as they never let go of one another, not in life nor in death. This garden was designed by a father and his beloved granddaughter.

All lovers searching for true love come and visit this site to be inspired by forever yours, in life or in death. This enchanted site sits amongst the flower havens. The sweet-smelling daffodils, roses, rosemary, thymes, sage, lilies, iris, violets, snowdrops, climbing jasmines, forget-me-nots, and water fountains all sit around a Madonna statue, blessing all visitors.

Upon arriving here, you shall be immersed within the heavenly sweet smells of Earthly flowers. Here, you shall find on a stone carved wall, a father's love letter to a daughter. May this unsaid, unread letter, be found throughout time as a gift with love to all daughters,

Dear Daughter,

Words are thoughts for me,

Never uttered,

Neither sung,

Nor have they been written,

Never expressed,

Never sent out,

Yet kept within

The interior stone

Wall of a father

Who never uttered

The word

Daughter,

So never heard

The blessed word

Papa,

Yet today, the unsaid words

Are written on a headstone

That says,

I am your beloved father

As you are my beloved daughter.

Forever my child,

Your Papa.

Signed,

Jacobus van Vrederic,

Father of Griet van Jacobus

Today, I have become a caretaker in a place where a swing is hung for true lovers to sit on. The swing says, "I shall never let you go" on her seat. Here, the rising phoenix has made a home where twin flames are known to rise from ashes. Here, flowers bloom spreading the sweet fragrances around the globe.

This is where a blessed love story had taken birth and never ended as love lives on forever. This sacred memorial sits by a river in the land, you all know as the Netherlands. This land had involved herself in a war to gain independence from Spain during my lifetime. I do hope by the time my diary ends up in your hands, we have become independent.

War washes away family members from houses across the land. It matters not which side you are on. She will, like the cold seawater, flood away all on her path. Only time will tell at what cost victory or defeat was attained, as she too tells her story.

If you are visiting this garden in the faraway future, then do respect all of whom have passed away to give you a free country. Today, my little granddaughter plants these small blue flowers and says with her little voice, "Grandfather, this is forget-me-not." She knows her mother had fought to bake bread for the soldiers of the war, and her father was an honorable soldier.

War rips through a land and brings freedom to all of her people. Do you ever wonder how many lives were affected by all the wars going on around the globe? How many families have been separated because of a war? A land finds her freedom and the future generations enjoy this freedom for the sacrifices made by the past generations. Today, wherever on Earth you may be, remember you are walking and living in peace as this freedom was brought to you through so many lives lost. Do remember all the lives lost during this time period.

Maybe you will one day walk into my home in Naarden and visit my child, grandchild, or my great grandchildren, who shall let you know to hold on to your beloved ones. Never let them go and do remind them every day, you love one another.

Forever, all of you are only one breath away from your beloved ones. So, love and cherish them with all your breath. For myself, I shall be here in Naarden, the Netherlands waiting for all of you to visit my granddaughter and me. I know when you do visit, you too will need a narrator.

I leave you with a note from my beloved daughter's diary. Maybe I will share more with you in the future. Today, I shall recite this to my beloved granddaughter. This is a poem written to me from her beloved mother,

Dear Papa,

I asked myself,

What is Papa?

I realized he is

The cold breeze of air,

In the hot summer's night.

I know he is

The hot burning heat,

During a cold snowy night.

When I am hungry,

He is the person

Who brings food on my table.

When I am lonely,

He is the friend I talk with.

When I am sad,

He is the voice of comfort I hear.

When I am happy,

He is the friend I play with.

When I grow up,

He will be there to hold on to me,

For when I wed

And bid my farewell,

He will cry and say,

My child shall never leave me.

I will then let him know,

Dear Papa,

I shall never let you go,

If only you were mine.

-Written by Griet van Jacobus

My daughter's poem will remain here. Her poem shall remain eternally as a love letter to a father. Within the walls of this garden, I have all my lost love found who are living through the flowers of this garden.

Yet I still have one last flower I need to find and bring back home to me. I shall plant her next to my tomb, if only I can find her. Till my last breath, I shall pursue this search, as my thirsty soul is dry and has not found the satisfaction in the unanswered questions of her final destination. Why does my soul say, you are still alive? We promised I would take my last breath watching you, as then you could take your last breath holding on to me.

My eyes will search for you eternally until I know where you are, Margriete van Wijck. Answer me, how my heart still beats, and your heart does not? This beloved of yours promises, forever you are my evermore beloved. A vow I had made I will keep, eternally beloved, I shall never let you go.

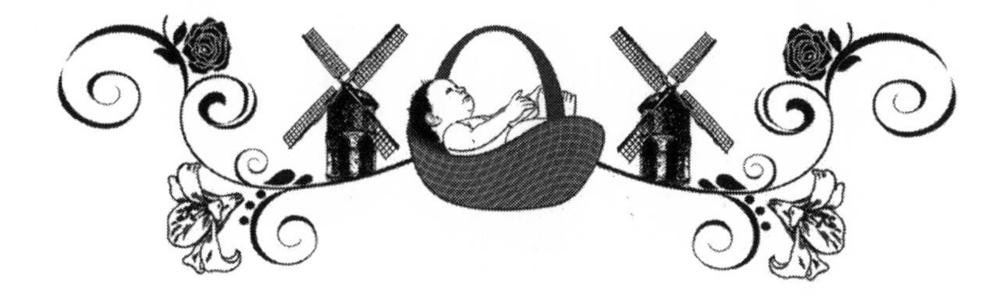

My Dear Readers,

Keep an eye out for the next book in the *Kasteel Vrederic* series, and find out how Jacobus keeps his given vow,

Evermore Beloved: I Shall Never Let You Go.

-Ann Marie Ruby

ABOUT THE AUTHOR

Ann Marie Ruby is an international number-one bestselling author. She has been a spiritual friend through her books. The bond between her readers and herself has been created through her books. You have all respected her privacy as she wanted to remain private, never questioned about her pictures, yet gave her your complete love without judging.

Some of you, the readers, had gone to the point where you too completely understood her request to remain private. The blessed readers around the globe have made Ann Marie's books bestsellers internationally. She has become from your love, an international number-one bestselling author.

This love that you poured to an unknown author had awakened her inner self and she wanted to give you her gift and reveal her face to this world. So, on the publication of her twelfth book, she revealed herself and became the known face giving you her blessings throughout time. All of you can see Ann Marie on her website and her social media pages.

If this world would have allowed, she would have distributed all of her books to you with her own hands as a gift and a message from a friend. She has taken pen to paper to spread peace throughout this Earth. Her sacred soul has found peace within herself as she says, "May I through my words bring peace and solace within your soul."

As many of you know, Ann Marie is also a dream psychic and a humanitarian. As a dream psychic, she has correctly predicted personal and global events. Some of these events have come true in front of us in the year 2020. She has also seen events from the past. You can read more about her journey as a dream psychic in *Spiritual Lighthouse: The Dream Diaries Of Ann Marie Ruby* which many readers have said is "the best spiritual book" they have read. As a humanitarian, she has taken pen to paper to end hate crimes within *The World Hate Crisis: Through The Eyes Of A Dream Psychic*.

To unite all race, color, and religion, following her dreams, Ann Marie has written two religiously unaffiliated prayer books, *Spiritual Songs: Letters From My Chest* and *Spiritual Songs II: Blessings From A Sacred Soul*, which people of all faiths can recite.

Ann Marie's writing style is known for making readers feel as though they have made a friend. She has written four books of original inspirational quotations which have also been compiled in one book, *Spiritual Ark: The Enchanted Journey Of Timeless Quotations*.

As a leading voice in the spiritual space, Ann Marie frequently discusses spiritual topics. As a spiritual person, she believes in soul families, reincarnation, and dreams. For this reason, she answers the unanswered questions of life surrounding birth, death, reincarnation, soulmates and twin flames, dreams, miracles, and end of time within her book *Eternal Truth: The Tunnel Of Light*. Readers have referred to this book as one of the must-read and most thought-provoking books.

The Netherlands has been a topic in various books by Ann Marie. As a dream psychic, she constantly has had dreams about this country before ever having any plan to visit the country or any previous knowledge of the contents seen within her dreams. Ann Marie's love and dreams of the Netherlands brought her to write *The Netherlands: Land Of My Dreams* which became an overnight number-one bestseller and topped international bestselling lists.

To capture not just the country but her past inhabitants, Ann Marie wrote for this country, *Everblooming: Through The Twelve Provinces Of The Netherlands*, a keepsake for all generations to come. This book also became an overnight number-one bestseller and topped international bestselling lists. Readers have called this book "the best book ever." They have asked for this book to be included in schools for all to read and cherish.

Love Letters: The Timeless Treasure is Ann Marie's thirteenth book. This book also became an overnight bestseller and topped international bestselling lists. Within this book, Ann Marie has gifted her readers fifty of her soul-touching love poems. She calls these poems, love letters. These are individual stories, individual love letters to a beloved, from a lover. In a poetic way, she writes to her twin flame. These poems are her gifts to all loving souls, all twin flames throughout time. All poems have an individual illustration retelling the stories, which Ann Marie designed herself.

Eternally Beloved: I Shall Never Let You Go is Ann Marie's fourteenth book. This is her first historical romance fiction, set within the Eighty Years' War-ravaged country, the Netherlands. You can travel through the eyes of Jacobus van Vrederic to the sixteenth century and find out how he battles time to find out love lives on even beyond time. His promise, however, is seen throughout the book and follows him to the sequel as he vows to his eternally beloved, "I shall never let you go."

Don't miss the sequel as the promise made by Jacobus to his beloved Margriete, continues to Ann Marie's next historical romance fiction, *Evermore Beloved: I Shall Never Let You Go*.

You have her name and know she will always be there for anyone who seeks her. Ann Marie's home is Washington State, USA, yet she travels all around the world to find you, the human with humanity.

Aside from her books, she loves writing blog posts and articles openly on her website. She has also interviewed award-winning individuals and organizations. Through the journey of her blog, she is available to all throughout this world. Come journey together and spread positivity, as she takes you on a positive journey through her website alongside her books. Remember you too can be a part of her journey.

For more information about Ann Marie Ruby, any one of her books, or to read her blog posts and articles, subscribe to her website, www.annmarieruby.com.

Follow Ann Marie Ruby on social media:

Twitter: @AnnahMariahRuby

Facebook: @TheAnnMarieRuby

Instagram: @Ann_Marie_Ruby

Pinterest: @TheAnnMarieRuby

BOOKS BY THE AUTHOR

INSPIRATIONAL QUOTATIONS SERIES:

This series includes four books of original quotations and one omnibus edition.

Spiritual Travelers:
Life's Journey From The Past
To The Present
For The Future

Spiritual
Messages:
From A Bottle

Spiritual Journey:
Life's Eternal Blessings

Spiritual
Inspirations:
Sacred Words
Of Wisdom

Omnibus edition contains all four books of original quotations.

Spiritual Ark:
The Enchanted Journey Of Timeless Quotations

SPIRITUAL SONGS SERIES:

This series includes two original spiritual prayer books.

SPIRITUAL SONGS: LETTERS FROM MY CHEST

When there was no hope, I found hope within these sacred words of prayers, I but call songs. Within this book, I have for you, 100 very sacred prayers.

SPIRITUAL SONGS II: BLESSINGS FROM A SACRED SOUL

Prayers are but the sacred doors to an individual's enlightenment. This book has 123 prayers for all humans with humanity.

SPIRITUAL LIGHTHOUSE: THE DREAM DIARIES OF ANN MARIE RUBY

Do you believe in dreams? For within each individual dream, there is a hidden message and a miracle interlinked. Learn the spiritual, scientific, religious, and philosophical aspects of dreams. Walk with me as you travel through forty nights, through the pages of my book.

THE WORLD HATE CRISIS: THROUGH THE EYES OF A DREAM PSYCHIC

Humans have walked into an age where humanity now is being questioned as hate crimes have reached a catastrophic amount. Let us in union stop this crisis. Pick up my book and see if you too could join me in this fight.

ETERNAL TRUTH: THE TUNNEL OF LIGHT

Within this book, travel with me through the doors of birth, death, reincarnation, true soulmates and twin flames, dreams, miracles, and the end of time.

THE NETHERLANDS: LAND OF MY DREAMS

Oh the sacred travelers, be like the mystical river and journey through this blessed land through my book. Be the flying bird of wisdom and learn about a land I call, Heaven on Earth.

EVERBLOOMING: THROUGH THE TWELVE PROVINCES OF THE NETHERLANDS

Original poetry and hand-picked tales are bound together in this keepsake book. Come travel with me as I take you through the lives of the Dutch past.

LOVE LETTERS: THE TIMELESS TREASURE

Fifty original timeless treasured love poems are presented with individual illustrations describing each poem.

KASTEEL VREDERIC SERIES:

ETERNALLY BELOVED: I SHALL NEVER LET YOU GO

Travel time to the sixteenth century where Jacobus van Vrederic, a beloved lover and father, surmounts time and tide to find the vanished love of his life. On his pursuit, Jacobus discovers secrets that will alter his life evermore. He travels through the Eighty Years' War-ravaged country, the Netherlands as he takes the vow, even if separated by a breath, "Eternally beloved, I shall never let you go."

Coming Soon

EVERMORE BELOVED: I SHALL NEVER LET YOU GO

EVERMORE BELOVED: I SHALL NEVER LET YOU GO

The second book in this series is coming soon.

Made in the USA
Las Vegas, NV
28 December 2023